Chapter 1

"What a cool baseball jersey!" Katie Carew complimented her best friend Jeremy Fox. It was Friday afternoon. Cherrydale Elementary School's fourth-graders had all just run out onto the playground for recess.

"Thanks," Jeremy said to Katie. "I got it yesterday when my dad and I were at the sporting-goods store in the mall. We were looking for a Mother's Day present for my mom."

"But *you* got the present," Katie pointed out.

"We bought one for my mom, too," Jeremy assured her.

"Do you really think your mom will want a baseball shirt for Mother's Day?" Suzanne Lock,

Katie's other best friend, asked Jeremy.

"She'll love it," Jeremy assured Suzanne. "My mom's a huge Cherrydale Porcupines fan."

Katie knew that was true. She'd been to baseball games with Mrs. Fox. Jeremy's mom screamed louder than anyone.

"If you say so," Suzanne told Jeremy. "I just know that my mom likes more girly presents for Mother's Day."

"Like what?" Jeremy asked.

"Every year I get her a big bouquet of roses," Suzanne told him.

"Speaking of roses . . ." George Brennan began with a big smile on his face. "How did the big rose greet the little rose?"

"How?" Katie asked him.

"Hi, Bud!" George exclaimed. He laughed at his own joke.

Katie laughed, too. She loved George's jokes.

But not everyone did. "That's so corny," Suzanne told him.

"You mean *thorny*," George corrected her. He started laughing all over again.

Suzanne rolled her eyes. "You know what your Mother's Day gift should be, George?" she asked.

"What?" George wondered.

"A day without jokes," Suzanne told him.

"My mom likes my jokes," George insisted. "Besides, we're taking her out for brunch for Mother's Day."

"Lucky you," George's best friend, Kevin

Camilleri, told him. "My big brother Ian and I have to *make* breakfast for my mom and then serve it to her in bed. It was my dad's idea."

"We tried that last year," Emma Weber told Kevin. "But the twins jumped in bed with my mom and spilled her tray. She spent the rest of Mother's Day washing her sheets and buying a new pillow because hers was soaked through with orange juice."

Katie could picture that. Emma W.'s twin brothers, Tyler and Timmy, were toddlers. They could be a real handful.

"So this year, we're just getting my mom a camera," Emma W. continued.

"My whole family is going to that new rock-climbing place for Mother's Day," Mandy Banks told the kids. "It was my mom's choice. She's always wanted to try it."

"Rock climbing sounds like a lot more fun than making toast and cereal," Kevin said with a frown. "I wish I had your mom!"

Katie gulped. Kevin had just done

something terrible. He'd made a wish!

"You do not wish that, Kevin!" she shouted. "You don't wish that at all."

The fourth-graders all stared at her.

"Katie Kazoo, what's with you?" George asked, using the way-cool nickname he'd given Katie in third grade.

Katie didn't know how to answer that. Her friends must have thought she'd gone nuts. But Katie *wasn't* nuts. She just knew that wishes didn't always come true the way you wanted them to.

Wishes could be bad, bad things.

Chapter 2

The whole wish mess had started one horrible day back in third grade. That day, Katie had lost the football game for her team. Then she'd splashed mud all over her favorite jeans. But the worst part was when Katie let out a loud burp—right in front of the whole class. Talk about embarrassing!

That night, Katie had wished she could be anyone but herself. There must have been a shooting star overhead when she made the wish, because the very next day the magic wind came.

The magic wind was like a really powerful tornado that blew around Katie and no one else. It was so strong, it could blow her right out of her body . . . *and into someone else's*!

The first time the magic wind appeared, it turned Katie into Speedy, the hamster who was the class pet. Katie spent the whole morning going around and around on a hamster wheel and chewing on Speedy's wooden chew sticks.

And that wasn't even the worst part. Things got *really* bad when she escaped from Speedy's cage and ran into the boys' locker room. That was when Katie landed inside George Brennan's stinky sneaker! *P.U.!* Katie sure was glad when the magic wind came back and switcherooed her into a kid again!

After that, the magic wind came again and again. One time it turned Katie into Kevin, right in the middle of his karate competition. Katie had tried to break a board in half with her foot. *Keeyah!* She'd missed the board completely and landed right on her rear end in front of everyone!

Another time, the magic wind turned Katie

into a clown fish at the Cherrydale Aquarium. She'd had a great time swimming around in the big tank—until a shark with huge, sharp teeth got a little too close! Katie was really glad when she changed back into a fourth-grader on dry land again!

Katie never knew when the magic wind would strike or who it would switcheroo her into. That was why Katie hated wishes so much. They only brought trouble. But she couldn't explain that to her friends. They wouldn't believe her, anyway. Katie wouldn't have believed it, either, if it didn't keep happening to her.

Still, she had to say *something*. Her friends were all staring at her.

"I just mean, you love your own mother, Kevin," Katie said quickly. "And you wouldn't trade her for anything."

"I guess," Kevin admitted. "But it *would* be fun to go rock climbing."

"I can't wait to go," Mandy told him. "They

put you in this harness thing and . . ."

Phew. Katie's friends were so interested in what Mandy was saying that they forgot how Katie had freaked out about Kevin's wish. That was one problem solved.

But Katie still had another big problem to deal with. She had no idea what to give her mom for Mother's Day. And that was just two days away.

Chapter 3

Unfortunately, Katie wasn't going to be able to solve that problem today. She had been hoping that her dad could take her shopping for a Mother's Day gift that evening. But when she got home, Katie found her grandmother waiting for her in the living room.

"Hi there, Kit-Kat," Katie's grandmother greeted her.

"Hi, Grandma," Katie said. "I didn't know you were coming over."

"Your dad had a late meeting, and your mom's busy at the bookstore tonight. So they called and asked me to come hang out with you," her grandmother explained.

Katie loved that her grandmother said they were hanging out together instead of calling it babysitting. After all, a fourth-grade girl was no baby.

"So what do you want to do?" her grandmother asked.

Katie shrugged. What she *had* wanted to do was go shopping at the mall. But Katie's grandmother didn't have a car. She rode a motorcycle. Katie wasn't allowed to ride on it.

"We could watch a movie or something," Katie suggested.

Her grandmother smiled. "Actually, I brought something even better," she said, pulling a few disks out of her backpack. "I just had some of my old home movies made into DVDs."

"Home movies?" Katie asked.

Her grandmother nodded. "Of your mother when she was a little girl."

Katie grinned. She loved hearing stories

about when her parents were little. But *seeing* her mom as a kid would be even more fun. "Great! Do you have any movies from when she was my age?"

Her grandmother searched through the DVDs, reading each of the labels. "She's about your age in this one," she said. "Let's pop it in."

"Speaking of pop . . . can we make some pop*corn*?" Katie asked. "We have it in the cabinet."

"Definitely," her grandmother agreed. "What's a movie without popcorn?"

* * *

A few minutes later, Katie and her grandmother were sitting on the couch with a big bowl of hot, buttery popcorn between them. Katie watched as a fuzzy image came onto the TV screen. It seemed to be a theater of some sort.

"Oh, I remember this," Katie's grandmother said with a smile. "It was Wendy's first tap-dancing recital."

"My mom tap dances?" Katie asked her.

"She used to," her grandmother explained. "She took lessons for a while. But when we moved to a new town, she stopped. There was only one dance school, and they didn't give tap classes. Oh, she was so sad."

That made Katie sad, too. She would hate to have to give up her cooking classes or her art classes because her family moved. Come to think of it, she wouldn't want to move at all.

Katie liked her neighborhood and her friends.

"Oh, look, the show is starting!" Katie's grandmother exclaimed.

Katie watched as the fourth-grade girls began tap dancing their way onto the stage. The first girl was wearing a big green tutu. Her crown had a green pointy thing coming out of the top.

"What's that?" Katie asked.

"It's supposed to be a stem," Katie's grandmother explained. "She's dressed as a green pepper."

"A what?" Katie asked, surprised.

"A pepper," Katie's grandmother repeated. "The girls were all supposed to be different vegetables in a salad."

Katie started to giggle. "A tap-dancing *salad*?"

Katie's grandmother laughed, too. "I know, it sounds silly. But they were so cute." She pointed to a girl in a purple tutu and crown. "She's supposed to be a cabbage."

The cabbage girl was followed by a dancer dressed in an orange leotard and tights. "She's a carrot, right?" Katie asked.

Her grandmother nodded. "Here comes your mom."

Sure enough, Katie's mother—or at least a fourth-grade version of her—flashed onto the screen. She was wearing red tights, a red tutu, and a red leotard.

"Mom's the tomato!" Katie exclaimed.

"Exactly," her grandmother replied.

Katie watched as her mom twirled around on the stage. "Mom was a pretty good tap dancer," Katie said.

"She was a *great* tap dancer," her grandmother corrected her. "Nothing made your mom happier than tap dancing back then. I felt really terrible when she had to give it up."

Suddenly Katie got one of her great ideas. She knew just what to get her mom for Mother's Day.

"I'm so glad you came over today, Grandma!" Katie exclaimed. She reached over and gave her grandmother a huge hug.

Whoops! The whole bowl of popcorn flipped over.

"Uh-oh!" Katie gulped.

"It's no big deal," her grandmother assured her. "I'll just get the vacuum."

"I don't think you'll need it." Katie giggled and pointed to the spilled popcorn. Her cocker spaniel, Pepper, was already eating it all up.

"I guess he was hungry," Katie's grandmother said. "Come to think of it, so am I. What do you want for dinner?"

Katie looked up at the TV screen. Katie's mom, the tomato, was tap dancing with the carrot, the pepper, and the cabbage.

"Suddenly I'm in the mood for a great big salad," she said with a giggle.

Chapter 4

"Happy Mother's Day!" Katie shouted as she bounded into the kitchen on Sunday morning.

"*Ruff! Ruff!*" Pepper barked as he followed Katie.

Mrs. Carew looked up from her coffee and began to laugh. "Thank you very much," she said. "Both of you."

Katie grinned. Pepper wagged his tail.

"This is for you." Katie put a big box down on the table.

"Wow!" Mrs. Carew exclaimed. "What a pretty bow. Did you wrap it yourself?"

Katie shook her head. "Daddy did it."

Mrs. Carew looked over at Katie's dad. "Great job," she complimented him.

"Thanks," he said.

By now, Katie was practically bursting with excitement. "Forget the wrapping paper. Open it!"

Mrs. Carew laughed as she tore the wrapping paper and opened the box. Then she looked inside. "Tap shoes?" she asked.

Katie nodded excitedly. "And Daddy and I went to Miss Ricky's School of Dance yesterday. We signed you up for tap-dancing classes."

"But why?" her mother asked.

"Grandma said you were really sad when you had to give up tap-dancing lessons," Katie explained. "Now you can take them again."

"That was a long time ago, Katie," Mrs. Carew said slowly.

Katie looked at her mom. "Don't you like my present?" she asked.

"Of course I do," Mrs. Carew assured Katie. She slipped the shoes on and tied the ribbons in bows.

"Do they fit?" Katie asked hopefully.

"Perfectly," her mother said. She stood up and began moving her feet back and forth.

The shoes made a swishing noise on the kitchen floor.

Then Katie's mom clicked her heel. *Tap.*

She pointed her toe. *Tap.*

Heel tap. Toe tap. Heel. Toe.

A big smile formed on Katie's mother's face. "I'd forgotten how much fun it was to tap dance," she said.

"Can you still do the tomato dance?" Katie asked her.

Katie's mom seemed surprised. "How did you know about that?" she asked.

"Grandma showed me the movie of your recital," Katie told her. "You were the best one in the whole salad!"

Katie's mom and dad started to laugh. So did Katie. That had sounded really funny.

Katie's mom twirled around in a little circle. "It will be so much fun to dance again!" she exclaimed.

Katie grinned. She'd done it! She'd given her mom the best Mother's Day present ever.

Chapter 5

Katie couldn't wait to tell her friends about the great gift she'd gotten for her mother. But when she walked into class 4A on Monday morning, she realized no one was thinking about Mother's Day anymore. The kids were all too curious about what had happened to their classroom.

Mr. Guthrie always decorated class 4A in a fun way. But this time, he'd gone absolutely crazy. There were maps everywhere.

When Katie looked up at the ceiling, she saw a big map of the North Pole.

When she looked down at the floor, she saw a map of the South Pole.

When she looked in front of her, she saw a map of Canada.

When she looked behind her, she saw a map of South America. It was kind of like standing in a giant globe.

"What in the world . . . ?" Emma Stavros began.

"Exactly." Mr. G. laughed.

"Are we studying foreign countries?" Kadeem Carter asked.

"Yes," Mr. G. agreed. "Also mountain ranges, rivers, oceans . . ."

"That's like studying the whole world," Andy Epstein said.

Mr. G. grinned. "Welcome to the world of geography!"

Huh? The kids all looked at their teacher strangely.

"Does anyone know what geography is?" Mr. G. asked the kids.

Emma W. raised her hand shyly. "It's a science," she said. "And it studies all the physical features of the Earth."

"That's right," Mr. G. told her with a smile. He turned to the rest of the class. "By the time we've finished this learning adventure, you'll all know the world a lot better. But before we can start, you dudes know what you have to do!"

"Decorate our beanbags!" Katie squealed excitedly.

"Exactly," Mr. G. told her. "So go to it!"

Katie ran over to the big box of decorations Mr. G. had left for the kids to use. She loved decorating her beanbag. It was one of the most fun things about being in class 4A.

The kids in Katie's classroom didn't sit at desks like other kids. Mr. G. thought kids learned better when they were comfortable. So they all sat in beanbag chairs. And every time they started a new learning adventure, the kids got to decorate them.

Katie had an especially good time decorating her beanbag this time. Last year, her family had been to Europe. They'd visited England, France, Spain, and Italy. So Katie decorated her beanbag with magazine pictures from each of those countries.

As she worked, Katie looked around at what the other kids were doing.

Emma S. had taped pictures of Hawaii all over her beanbag. She'd even made a newspaper palm tree.

Kevin was busy using blocks to build the Great Wall of China all around his beanbag.

Kadeem had covered the sides of his beanbag with blue and green tissue paper. Now he was drawing fish all over it. Katie figured he was making an ocean.

George's beanbag was the strangest one in the whole class. So far, all he'd done was cover it with white paper and cotton balls.

"What are you doing?" Katie asked him.

"My beanbag's the North Pole," George told her. "There's nothing up there but ice and snow."

"That's not exactly true, George," Mr. G. told him. "There are mountains, water, and other landforms up there. You'll have to learn all about that before our Geography Bee."

"Our what?" Mandy asked.

"Geography Bee," Mr. G. repeated. "It's like a spelling bee. But instead of spelling words, you'll be asked questions about geography. The whole fourth grade is going to be participating."

"Let's make sure the winner is from our class!" Mandy declared.

"Definitely," Andy agreed.

Katie knew Mandy and Andy were going to

study really hard to win the Geography Bee. Winning was very important to both of them.

Then again, winning was important to a lot of kids in class 4B, too. Especially Suzanne and Jeremy. Katie figured they were going to work hard to make sure no one in Katie's class won the Geography Bee. If that happened and class 4B wound up winning, Suzanne would never let Katie—or anyone else in class 4A—forget it!

The thought of that made Katie want to work extra hard.

"Hurry up, you guys, finish decorating," Katie urged her classmates. "We have to get studying. It's a big world out there!"

Chapter 6

"Thanks for inviting me to study at your house, Katie," Emma W. said as the girls walked home together after school that afternoon. "It's so noisy at my house."

Katie nodded. She knew what Emma W. meant. Emma W. had three younger brothers and a teenage sister. Someone was always screaming, crying, or talking on the phone at her house. But Katie was an only child. It was always nice and quiet at the Carew house.

"I checked this atlas out of the library today," Katie said, holding up a big book. "It's got maps and facts about every country in the world."

"Awesome," Emma W. said. "We can make note cards with facts on them and test each other."

"Great idea!" Katie agreed.

Katie's mom was in the kitchen when the girls walked in. She was wearing a leotard and her tap shoes.

"Mom, you were dancing today!" Katie exclaimed happily.

"I just got home from my first lesson," Mrs. Carew told the girls. "It was so much fun!"

"I knew you'd love it," Katie told her.

"Why don't you girls sit down? I'll fix you a snack before you do your homework," Katie's mom suggested.

"Thanks," Katie said. "Please make it a really big snack. We need lots of energy to memorize geography facts."

"That's true," Emma W. agreed. "But maybe we should study while we eat so we don't waste any time."

"Great idea!" Katie told her. She sat down at the kitchen table and opened up her atlas. "Let's start with Africa."

As the girls read about the Aberdare mountain range in Kenya, Mrs. Carew busied herself getting the girls cookies and milk. Even when she walked over to the refrigerator, her tap shoes clicked and clacked on the floor.

"Heel tap, ball tap, shuffle," Mrs. Carew murmured to herself. "Heel tap, ball tap . . ."

Katie smiled. Her mom was dancing in the kitchen. She'd had so much fun in class, she didn't want to stop now.

"That's pretty good, Mom," she told her.

"It's coming back to me," her mom agreed.

"Tap dancing looks like a lot of fun," Emma W. said.

"It is," Mrs. Carew replied.

A few minutes later, when the girls had

finished their snacks, they went into the living room. There was plenty of room for them both to look at the big atlas and to start making their note cards.

The only trouble was, the living room was right near the kitchen. And the kitchen was where Katie's mom was.

Click, clack. Tap, tap. Click, clack. Tap, tap.

"Your mom sure loves tap dancing," Emma W. told Katie.

"I know," Katie agreed. "Those lessons were the best gift I ever got her."

Tap, tap. Click, clack.

Katie tried hard to focus on the map of Africa in the atlas, but the noise was making it hard.

"Ruff! Ruff!"

Oh, no! Now Pepper was barking along with the tapping.

Tap, tap.

"Ruff! Ruff!"

Finally Emma W. looked over at Katie. "I

think I'm going to go home," she said in her sweet, kind voice. "I'm having a little trouble studying."

"I know what you mean," Katie agreed.

Emma W. picked up her book bag and started to laugh. "You know, I never thought any place could be noisier than my house," she said.

Katie listened to the tapping and the barking coming from the kitchen. "I never did, either," she told Emma W. "But today my house wins!"

* * *

Katie was sitting on the front porch when her dad's car pulled up in the driveway that evening.

"What are you doing out here?" her dad asked her.

"Studying geography," Katie answered.

"Outside?" He sounded surprised. "It's getting kind of dark."

"I know," Katie agreed. "But it's too noisy to study inside. Mom's tap dancing. And Pepper is barking a lot."

"Oh." Mr. Carew sat down next to Katie. "Well, at least you know Mom liked your gift." He looked down at the atlas Katie had been studying. "Geography, huh? That was always my favorite subject."

"We're having a Geography Bee next week,"

Katie told her dad. "I'm trying to learn as much as I can."

"An atlas is great," Mr. Carew agreed. "But I have another book upstairs that might help you, too."

"Ooh! Let's go get it!" Katie pleaded.

"After dinner," her dad promised.

"Do you think Mom will stop dancing long enough to eat?" Katie asked him.

Mr. Carew shrugged. "If not, we'll have a show to watch with our dinner," he joked. "Just like when we saw that flamenco dancer in Spain."

Katie gulped. She remembered that show. That was the time the magic wind turned her into a flamenco dancer. She'd fallen off the stage and splashed rice and seafood all over the audience. What a mess!

She sure hoped tonight's dinner would be more peaceful than that!

Chapter 7

But dinnertime was just as noisy as the afternoon had been.

First, Katie's mom tapped from the oven to the table with the vegetarian lasagna.

Then she twirled from the refrigerator to the table with the milk.

Finally she shuffle-stepped from the counter to the table with the chocolate cake.

"This dinner sure was tip-top," Mr. Carew told Katie's mom.

"Tip-top *tap*," Katie joked.

Katie's mom curtsied. "Thank you, my adoring fans," she joked.

✦ ✦ ✦

After dinner, Katie and her dad went upstairs to look at his special geography book.

"I really want to do well in the Geography Bee," Katie told her dad. "Maybe I'll even win."

"You can try," Mr. Carew answered. "And this will definitely help."

Katie's dad pulled a big black binder from the top of a bookshelf. He opened it to a page in the middle.

Katie looked at the book. She was a little confused. "Stickers?" she asked. "How can a sticker book help me win the Geography Bee?"

Mr. Carew shook his head. "Look closer," he said. "They're *not* stickers. They're stamps."

"They're not like any stamps I've ever seen," Katie told him.

"That's because they're from different countries," her dad explained. "See that one with the ballerina painting on it? It's from France. The colorful one with the horse and carriage is from China. And the one in the corner with Noah's Ark is from Israel."

"This is so cool!" Katie exclaimed. "I didn't know you collected stamps."

"I started when I was about your age," her dad told her. "It's a lot of fun. I used to imagine I lived in all these different places."

"Where's that red one with the boat on it from?" Katie asked.

Mr. Carew looked closely at the stamp. "New Guinea," he said.

"Where's that?" Katie asked him.

"I'll show you," her dad answered. He turned the page and showed Katie a map of the world. There were stamps all over the map. "I tried to put the stamps on the countries they came from." He pointed to an island in the middle of the Pacific Ocean. "See, there's another copy of that stamp. And that's where New Guinea is."

"This is great," Katie said.

Mr. Carew nodded. "You can look at it for as long as you like," he told Katie. "I have a lot of other albums, too. Just be careful. A lot of these stamps are kind of old."

"You can count on me, Dad," Katie told him. "I won't let anything happen to your stamps. I promise!"

Chapter 8

A few days later, Katie and Emma W. went to the Cherrydale Mall after school. Katie's mom was the manager of the Book Nook bookstore. Katie had been coming to the mall since she was a little kid. Nearly everyone who worked there knew her.

"You want to go have a pizza at Louie's?" Katie asked Emma W. "I can ask him to make my favorite veggie pizza."

"Yum!" Emma W. exclaimed. "We can study our geography flash cards while we eat. I want to go over the Asian countries again."

Katie walked to the front of the bookstore,

where her mom was hanging a poster on the wall.

"We're going to Louie's for some pizza and studying," Katie told her mom.

"Great idea," Mrs. Carew said. She stepped back and looked at her poster. "Does that look straight to you?" she asked the girls.

Emma W. nodded. "What is a Tap-Off?" she asked, reading the poster.

"It's an event that Miss Ricky's dance school is having," Katie's mom explained. "We're trying to get as many people as we can to tap dance in the parking lot outside the mall. Our goal is to break a record for the most people tap dancing at one time."

"Why are you doing that?" Katie asked her.

"Miss Ricky wants to get people interested in tap dancing," her mother explained. "Hopefully, newspaper and TV reporters will come and do stories about the Tap-Off. Then people will want to take lessons."

"Cool," Emma W. said. "Can I be one of the

dancers? I mean, I've never taken tap dancing, but . . ."

"Of course you can dance with us. Miss Ricky is going to teach the routine to everyone," Katie's mom told Emma W. "Also, a few of the dancers from Miss Ricky's school will be at the front of the crowd. You can watch them and follow what they do. I'm trying out to be one of those dancers."

"Cool! You could be on TV," Katie said.

"If I'm chosen," her mom replied. "I hope I'm good enough."

"I'm sure you are," Emma W. told her. "Katie says all you do is practice tap dancing."

Mrs. Carew gave Katie a funny look, but she didn't say anything.

"Are you ready to go to Louie's now?" Katie asked Emma W.

"Sure," Emma W. told her. "Good-bye, Mrs. Carew."

"Bye, Emma," Mrs. Carew answered. "I'll see you at the Tap-Off."

"You sure will," Emma W. said.

"Bye, Mom," Katie said.

"See you later, Katie," Mrs. Carew called after her.

As the girls walked out of the store, Emma W. asked Katie, "Are you going to dance in the Tap-Off?"

Katie shook her head. "I don't think so."

"Don't you think it's great that your mom is going to audition to be one of the dancers who gets to be on TV?" Emma W. asked.

"No," Katie said.

"Why?" Emma W. wondered.

"Because that's going to mean I'll have to hear a lot more tap-tap-tapping," Katie told her.

⭐ ⭐ ⭐

A few minutes later, Katie and Emma W. were sitting in a booth at Louie's Pizza Shop. They were sipping orange sodas and waiting for their veggie pizza with extra broccoli.

Emma W. held up a flash card. "The Yellow River is on which continent?" she asked.

"That's easy," Katie said. "Asia. It's in China."

"Exactly right," Emma W. told her.

Now it was Katie's turn to hold up a flash card. "Fiji is an island in which ocean?"

"The Pacific Ocean," Emma W. answered.

"You got it!" Katie exclaimed. "My dad has the coolest stamp from Fiji. It has pretty yellow mushrooms on it."

Just then, Suzanne and her mom walked into Louie's. Suzanne was carrying a lot of shopping bags. Her mom looked very tired.

"Wow! You've been busy," Katie said to Suzanne.

"I'm studying," Suzanne explained.

Katie and Emma W. looked at her strangely.

"How is shopping studying?" Emma W. wondered.

Suzanne pulled a pink cap out of one bag. "This would keep me warm in Antarctica, which is near the South Pole."

Katie doubted a little cotton cap would

be much help in Antarctica, but she didn't say anything.

Suzanne held up a bathing suit next. "If I were in the Amazon rain forest, where it's very hot, I'd need this."

"It's actually for Suzanne to wear this summer," Mrs. Lock told Katie and Emma W.

Suzanne scowled at her mom. "Right now, it's for studying," she insisted. "I've been studying hard for the Geography Bee. I'm planning on winning."

"So are we," Katie told Suzanne. "In fact, we're studying right now."

Suzanne looked around. "Where are your packages?" she asked.

Katie and Emma W. started to laugh.

"Only you could turn a Geography Bee into a fashion show, Suzanne," Katie said.

Just then, Louie brought the veggie pizza over to the table. Katie and Emma W. offered Suzanne and her mother a slice.

Suzanne folded her slice in half and started to

take a bite. A big glob of tomato-covered cheese fell on her shirt.

"Oh, no!" Suzanne moaned.

"Don't worry, Suzanne," Katie said. "Pizza is from Italy. Now you have an Italian shirt. It's studying!"

Suzanne gave Katie a funny look. Then she smiled. "You're right. And Italy is a country that's shaped like a boot. Boots are in fashion these days."

"I wonder if that will be a question in the Geography Bee," Emma W. teased.

"If it is, I'm ready!" Suzanne exclaimed happily as she took a big bite of her Italian pizza.

Chapter 9

Tap. Shuffle. Stomp.

That was pretty much all Katie heard for
the next few days as her mom practiced for
her big audition. It was kind of annoying, but
Katie had to admit that her mom was becoming
a really good dancer.

"You're definitely going to be picked to be
in the front at the Tap-Off," Katie told her mom
as the two of them walked into the studio on
Saturday for the audition.

"I hope so," Mrs. Carew replied. "I've been
practicing really hard. I think I have the whole
routine memorized."

Katie was sure her mom had the routine

memorized. After seeing it over and over again, *Katie* practically knew the whole thing by heart.

"I'm so glad you came with me today," Katie's mom continued. "It will help me a lot to see you sitting there."

Katie tried to smile. She was glad she could be there to support her mom. But part of her also really wished she didn't have to see—or hear—any more tap dancing.

Katie followed her mother into a large dance studio. "You can sit over there," Katie's mom said, pointing to a row of chairs. "I'm going to warm up."

Katie sat down in one of the chairs and watched the dancers stretch their arms and legs. But after a few minutes, Katie got a little squirmy. She got up to walk around a bit.

Actually, Miss Ricky's School of Dance was kind of a neat place. There were lots of studios. But everyone was in the big studio where the auditions were being held.

Katie wandered into one of the smaller studios. It was empty. She looked at herself in the mirror. She pointed her toe. Then she tapped her foot and twirled around. It was hard *not* to dance in a room like this. But Katie was glad no one was there to see her. She was definitely not as good a dancer as her mom was.

Just then, Katie felt a cool breeze blowing on the back of her neck. That was weird. There were no windows in the studio. And the fan wasn't turned on.

Where was the breeze coming from?

The breeze turned into a wind and began blowing colder and harder until it was like a wild tornado. *A tornado that was spinning only around Katie.*

Oh, no! This wasn't an ordinary wind. It was the magic wind. And boy, was it blowing. The wind was so fierce, Katie was afraid it might blow her all the way to the continent of Asia or even Antarctica! Katie shut her eyes tight and tried not to cry.

And then it stopped. Just like that. The magic wind was gone.

So was Katie Kazoo. She'd been turned into someone else. One, two, switcheroo!

The question was, who?

✫ ✫ ✫

Katie stood there a minute with her eyes shut. All around her, she heard the tap-tap-tapping of dancers in tap shoes.

That was weird. A moment ago, she was alone in the little studio. The magic wind had blown her back into the big studio. As she opened her eyes, Katie saw lots of dancers all around her. The only one she didn't see was her mom.

At least not at first. But as she turned around, Katie spotted her mom's reflection in the mirror. Mrs. Carew seemed to be standing in the middle of the room with a confused look on her face.

Katie tried to smile in her mom's direction to make her feel more confident.

Her mom gave Katie the same exact smile.

Katie waved at her mom in the mirror.

Her mom waved to Katie at the exact same time.

Katie looked down at her feet. She was wearing tap shoes!

Tap . . . tap . . . shuffle. Katie moved her feet back and forth.

Tap . . . tap . . . shuffle. The mom in the mirror moved her feet back and forth.

Uh-oh! That could only mean one thing. Katie had turned into her mom—right before the big audition! Katie had to get out of there. *Right away*. She turned and started to run out of the studio. The heels on her tap shoes went *clickety clack, clickety clack* as she ran.

But it was too late.

"Okay, dancers," Miss Ricky announced. "It's time to start the auditions. First on our list is Wendy Carew."

Katie gulped. This was soooo not good!

Chapter 10

Katie wanted to run and hide somewhere until the magic wind came to turn her back into a fourth-grade girl. But she knew she couldn't do that. Not now. Her mother had been practicing all week for this audition. Katie had to at least *try* and help her out.

So Katie took her place in the middle of the dance floor. She stood tall as Miss Ricky put the CD in the player. And then the music started. Katie knew the song right away. It was an old tune called "That's Entertainment." Her mom had played it over and over as she practiced.

"Toe. Heel. Ball change," Katie whispered

to herself as she moved her feet the way she'd seen her mother do it. "Hop. Toe. Stomp."

Katie smiled. She was really getting the feel of it. And so far, the routine was going okay. She even thought she saw Miss Ricky smile back at her.

Ball change. Heel. Toe. Spin.

Katie began to spin around the way she'd seen her mother twirl in the kitchen. She tapped her toes a little faster as she turned, keeping in time with the music.

Heel. Toe. Spin.

Whoa. Suddenly Katie started to feel dizzy. She stopped spinning. But the room didn't. Everything seemed to be turning around and around, even though Katie was standing still.

Katie tried to keep dancing. She moved across the dance floor tapping her feet. But the room kept spinning.

Whoops! Katie tripped over her right foot. She fell right on her rear end.

At first, no one said anything. Then a few of

the dancers began to giggle—quietly, like they were trying not to hurt Katie's feelings.

But Katie heard them. And her feelings *were* hurt. She was really embarrassed.

"Are you okay, Wendy?" Miss Ricky asked her.

Wendy! Katie had almost forgotten that she wasn't Katie anymore. She was her mom. That made things even worse.

Tears began streaming down Katie's face. She had to get out of that awful dance studio right away!

"I'm fine." Katie sobbed as she ran out of the room.

* * *

A moment later, Katie was sitting all by herself on the floor of one of the empty studios.

"I sure made a mess of things this time," Katie whispered sadly to herself.

Just then, Katie felt a cool breeze blowing on the back of her neck. And before she even had a chance to look for an open window or a fan, the breeze grew into a strong wind. A second later, it was a tornado that was blowing just around Katie.

The magic wind had returned!

The wind began to spin faster and faster. It whirled around Katie so powerfully, she was sure it would blow her away.

And then it stopped. Just like that. Katie Kazoo was back!

So was her mom. And boy, did she look confused.

"How did I get into this room?" Katie's mom asked.

"You came in here after I . . . I mean after you . . ." Katie began. She wasn't really sure what to say.

Mrs. Carew rubbed her rear end. "I'm really sore," she complained. "I feel like I fell on my . . ." She stopped for a minute. "I *did* fall, didn't I?"

Katie nodded.

"Wow," Mrs. Carew continued. "I kind of remember getting dizzy out there after my spin, but it's all sort of fuzzy."

"You started out really great," Katie assured her.

"That audition was a disaster," Mrs. Carew told Katie. She frowned sadly. "I think maybe it's time for me to find a new hobby."

Now Katie felt really awful. "You can't stop dancing," she told her mom.

Mrs. Carew smiled at Katie. "I know you wanted me to have fun with my gift," she said. "And I did. But I'm just not a very good dancer anymore."

"Yes, you are," Katie told her. "I just started to spin too fast."

"You what?" her mom asked.

Oops. "I mean *you* were just spinning fast," Katie corrected herself. "That's why you got dizzy."

Katie's mother sighed and shook her head. "Come on," she said. "Let's go home. I need to get out of this place."

Chapter 11

The next day it was very quiet at Katie's house. There was no tapping, stomping, or clapping. It was the perfect place to study. That made Katie very sad.

"Your mom's not going to dance at all anymore?" Emma W. asked her. She and George had come over to look at some of Katie's dad's stamp albums.

Katie shook her head. "Mom put the tap shoes away. She says she's looking for a new hobby."

"She should try archery," George suggested. "That's my dad's hobby. He's teaching *me* how to shoot arrows now."

"That's really cool," Emma W. said.

"Archery is an Olympic sport," George said.

"The Olympics started in Greece," Emma W. told him. "And Greece is located in what sea?"

"The Mediterranean!" George exclaimed happily.

"You got it," Emma W. said with a smile.

Katie wished she could be as interested as her friends were in geography. But right now all she could think about was how her mom had stopped dancing—and how it had all been Katie's fault.

"I have to get going," Emma W. said. "I promised my mom I'd be home early today."

"I guess I should go home, too," George said. "But this has been great. Those stamps really make studying geography fun. You should bring one of your dad's stamp albums to school tomorrow. Then everyone in our class can study with it."

"I don't know . . ." Katie began.

"It would totally give our class an advantage

over 4B, Katie Kazoo," George said. "That stamp album would be our secret weapon!"

Katie thought about that. "I guess I could bring one album," she said. "But just for tomorrow."

"Bring the one with stamps from South America," Emma W. suggested. She slipped on a little pink sweater.

"That's pretty," Katie told her.

"Thanks," Emma W. replied. "My mom and I made it together. She's teaching me how to knit."

"Cool," Katie said.

"It's fun," Emma W. said. "And it's something special I do with my mom. She doesn't knit with anyone else. Not my sister Lacey or any of my brothers."

Katie knew that must make Emma W. really happy. With so many kids in her house, it was hard for Emma W. to get special time with her mom.

Suddenly a big smile flashed on Katie's face.

Hooray! Katie Kazoo had just gotten one of her great ideas!

* * *

Tap . . . tap. . . shuffle.

The next morning, Katie danced her way into class 4A.

"What are you doing?" Emma W. asked her.

"Tap dancing," Katie explained. "My mom is teaching me."

"I thought you said your mom wasn't taking tap-dancing lessons anymore," Emma W. said.

"She isn't," Katie said. "But I asked her if she could teach *me* to dance. I thought it could be our special hobby. Like the way you and your mom knit. And George and his dad do archery."

"Cool," Emma W. said.

"My mom taught me a few steps," Katie said. "We might even make up a dance together. Tap dancing is fun."

"Are you going to be in the Tap-Off?" Emma W. asked her.

Katie shrugged. "My mom still doesn't want

to. But maybe she'll change her mind."

Just then, George walked over to where and Emma W. and Katie were sitting. "Did you bring the secret weapon?" he asked her.

Katie patted her backpack. "It's right here. We have to be careful with it. My dad would be really upset if anything happened to his stamps."

George smiled. "The stamp album will be fine," he said. "What could happen?"

Chapter 12

Katie could lose the stamp album. *That* was what could happen.

"This is soooo not good," Katie told a group of her friends during lunch. "I promised my dad that I wouldn't let anything happen to any of his stamps, and now I've lost a whole book of them!"

"Calm down," Emma W. said. "They couldn't have just disappeared. When did you have them last?"

"I don't remember," Katie told her. "I had them in the classroom early in the morning. And you and I were looking at them in the library. But after that, I'm not sure."

"We'll just have to go everywhere you went today and look for them," George said.

"But I was all over the school," Katie said. "The library, the gym, our classroom. I was in the bathroom, too. Twice."

Kevin took out a piece of paper and a pen.

"What are you doing?" Katie asked him.

"I'm drawing a map of the school," Kevin explained. "We'll follow the map and look for the book during recess."

"But recess is so short," Katie said. "We won't have time to search the whole school."

"That's okay," Kevin said. "I'm splitting the map into four parts. I'll look in the north part of the school. George will look in the south. Emma will look in the east, and you can look west."

"School geography!" George exclaimed.

"This will be fun!" Emma W. added.

Katie sighed. She didn't care if school geography was fun. She just wanted it to work.

* * *

Right after the kids finished their lunch, they started their search. Katie raced to the west side of the school. First, she stopped in the girls' room, where she'd gone just before gym.

She searched all the stalls, but the stamp album wasn't there.

Then she ran into the gym, where class 4A had played class 4B in basketball . . . and lost. No, the stamp album wasn't there, either.

Finally, Katie went into the library. That was

the last place she actually remembered looking at the stamp album.

"Hi, Katie," Ms. Folio, the school librarian, greeted her. "Have you come to spend recess in the library?"

Katie shook her head. "I'm looking for my dad's stamp album. Have you seen it?"

"No," Ms. Folio said. "Are you sure you had it in here?"

"Yes," Katie assured her. "Emma and I were looking at it at the table near the window."

Ms. Folio thought for a minute. "Mr. Keaton's first-grade class was in here right after your class left. Maybe one of the first-graders saw it."

"Do you think Mr. Keaton would let me ask the kids if they did?" Katie asked. "It's very important. My dad will be so upset if I don't get his stamps back."

"I'm sure Mr. Keaton will let you look for the stamp album." Ms. Folio looked up at the clock. "The first grade is having a snack now.

They should be in their classroom."

"Thanks, Ms. Folio," Katie said as she dashed out of the library and ran farther west down the hall to Mr. Keaton's room.

✦ ✦ ✦

The first-graders were having crackers and milk when Katie knocked on Mr. Keaton's door.

"Katie," Mr. Keaton greeted her. "What a surprise. Why aren't you out on the playground with the other fourth-graders?"

"I lost something important," Katie told him. "I'm spending recess looking for it. Ms. Folio said one of your kids might have seen it."

"What did you lose?" Mr. Keaton asked.

"My dad's stamp album," Katie told him. "It's a black binder filled with pages of stamps."

"Did any of you see a black binder?" Mr. Keaton asked his class.

A small girl with a head of blond curls raised her hand shyly. "I found a binder in the library." She pulled it out of her desk.

"That's it!" Katie exclaimed happily.

"This binder has lots of stickers," the little girl said.

"That's what I thought at first, too," Katie said. "But they're really stamps from other countries."

Katie showed the little girl a few of the stamps. Then she took the binder, thanked Mr. Keaton, and raced off to tell her friends that she'd found the album.

Tap . . . tap . . . tap.

Katie was so happy, she danced the whole way!

Chapter 13

Katie was still tap-tap-tapping on Saturday morning when she and her mother arrived at the Cherrydale Mall for the big Tap-Off.

"Mrs. Carew!" Emma W. exclaimed when she saw them. "I thought you weren't going to dance in the Tap-Off."

Katie's mom shrugged. "I guess I realized that the Tap-Off is about showing people how great tap dancing is, not about being in the front of the crowd."

"My mom's here with me," Emma W. told Katie and her mom. "And Lacey."

Katie was surprised to see Emma W.'s teenage sister. She hardly ever did anything with Emma W.

"Hi, Wendy," Mrs. Weber greeted Katie's mom. "Emma told us about this and we just had to come. Tap dancing sounds like such a fun mother-daughter thing to do."

"It is!" Katie's mom assured her. "In fact, Katie and I have been talking to Miss Ricky about starting a mother-daughter class."

"We would definitely sign up," Mrs. Weber replied. "I could use the exercise, and it would be fun for the girls."

"I'm so glad you didn't give up on tap dancing, Mrs. Carew," Emma W. said.

"I have Katie to thank for that," Katie's mom said. "She convinced me to stick with it. And with some hard work, I'm going to get better and better."

"Hard work always pays off," Katie said. "That's how Emma won our Geography Bee yesterday!"

"Congratulations, Emma," Mrs. Carew said.

"You should have seen how mad Suzanne

was that someone from 4B didn't win," Katie told her mom. "She almost popped a button on her lederhosen!"

"Lederhosen?" Mrs. Carew asked.

"You know, those leather shorts kids wear in Germany," Emma W. explained. "Suzanne was wearing them to help her study Europe."

Mrs. Carew giggled. "Suzanne is one of a kind," she said.

Just then loud music began blaring through the parking lot.

"Let's dance," Mrs. Carew cheered.

Toe. Heel. Ball change. Spin.

As she twirled around, Katie grinned happily. Despite everything, Katie's mom was still dancing and having a great time. And so was Katie.

Take that, magic wind!

A World of Record Breakers!

Katie and her friends are really world-class geography experts! Now they're sharing a whole world of fun facts with you!

⭐ The world's highest mountain is Mount Everest. At its highest point, the mountain is more than 29,000 feet above sea level!

⭐ The lowest spot on land is the Dead Sea in Israel. It's located over 1,300 feet *below* sea level.

The largest ocean is the Pacific Ocean, which covers about thirty percent of the planet! It covers more than sixty million square miles.

The smallest ocean is the Arctic Ocean. It covers less than six million square miles of the planet. That is only about three percent of the Earth's surface.

Australia is the world's smallest continent. It's almost three million square miles, which is actually smaller than the country of Brazil.

The world's largest continent is Asia. More than three billion people live there.

About the Author

Nancy Krulik is the author of more than 150 books for children and young adults, including three *New York Times* best sellers. She lives in New York City with her husband, composer Daniel Burwasser, their children, Amanda and Ian, and Pepper, a chocolate and white spaniel mix. When she's not busy writing the *Katie Kazoo, Switcheroo* series, Nancy loves swimming, reading, and going to the movies.

About the Illustrators

John & Wendy have illustrated all of the *Katie Kazoo* books, but when they're not busy drawing Katie and her friends, they like to paint, take photographs, travel, and play music in their rock 'n' roll band. They live and work in Brooklyn, New York.